to Pete and Dilly, fellow bird watchers

HENNY

Retold and Illustrated by

PAUL GALDONE

PENNY

The Seabury Press New York

Copyright © 1968 by Paul Galdone. Library of Congress Catalog Card Number: 68-24735. ISBN: 0-8164-3022-5. Printed in the United States of America. *Fourth Printing*.

ONE day when Henny Penny
was scratching among the leaves,
an acorn fell out of a tree
and struck her on the head.

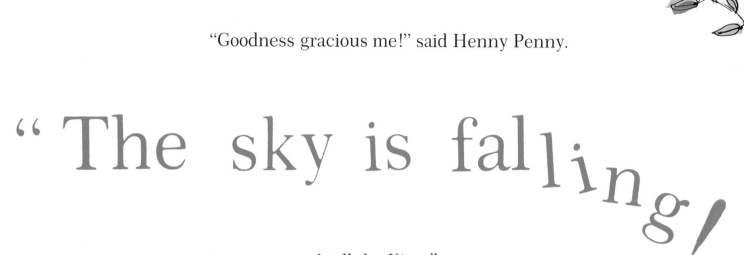

"Goodness gracious me!" said Henny Penny.

"The sky is falling!

I must go and tell the King."

So she went along and she went along and she went along, until she met Cocky Locky.

"Cock-a-doodle-doo! Where are you going, Henny Penny?" asked Cocky Locky.

"Oh," said Henny Penny, "the sky is falling and I am going to tell the King."

"May I go with you, Henny Penny?" asked Cocky Locky.

"Yes, indeed," said Henny Penny.

So Henny Penny and Cocky Locky went off to tell the King that the sky was falling.

They went along and they went along and they went along, until they met Ducky Lucky.

"Quack, quack, quack! Where are you going, Henny Penny and Cocky Locky?" asked Ducky Lucky.

"Oh, we are going to tell the King that the sky is falling," said Henny Penny and Cocky Locky.

"May I go with you?" asked Ducky Lucky.

"Yes, indeed," said Henny Penny and Cocky Locky.

So Henny Penny, Cocky Locky, and Ducky Lucky went off to tell the King that the sky was falling.

They went along and they went along and they went along, until they met Goosey Loosey.

"Honk, honk, honk! Where are you going, Henny Penny, Cocky Locky, and Ducky Lucky?" asked Goosey Loosey.

"Oh, we are going to tell the King that the sky is falling," said Henny Penny, Cocky Locky, and Ducky Lucky.

"May I go with you?" asked Goosey Loosey.

"Yes, indeed," said Henny Penny, Cocky Locky, and Ducky Lucky.

So Henny Penny, Cocky Locky, Ducky Lucky, and Goosey Loosey went off to tell the King that the sky was falling.

They went along and they went along and they went along, until they met Turkey Lurkey.

"Gobble, gobble, gobble!" said Turkey Lurkey. "Where are you going, Henny Penny, Cocky Locky, Ducky Lucky, and Goosey Loosey?"

"Oh, we are going to tell the King that the sky is falling," said Henny Penny, Cocky Locky, Ducky Lucky, and Goosey Loosey.

"May I go with you?" asked Turkey Lurkey.

"Yes, indeed," said Henny Penny, Cocky Locky, Ducky Lucky, and Goosey Loosey.

So Henny Penny, Cocky Locky, Ducky Lucky, Goosey Loosey, and Turkey Lurkey went off to tell the King that the sky was falling.

They went along and they went along and they went
along, until they met Foxy Loxy.

"Where are you going, Henny Penny, Cocky Locky,
Ducky Lucky, Goosey Loosey, and Turkey Lurkey?" asked
Foxy Loxy.

"Oh, we are going to tell the King that the sky is falling,"
said Henny Penny, Cocky Locky, Ducky Lucky, Goosey
Loosey, and Turkey Lurkey.

"Ah, ha!" said Foxy Loxy. "But this isn't the way to the King, Henny Penny, Cocky Locky, Ducky Lucky, Goosey Loosey, and Turkey Lurkey. Come with me and I will show you a shortcut to the King's palace."

"Oh, good!" said Henny Penny, Cocky Locky, Ducky Lucky, Goosey Loosey, and Turkey Lurkey.

They went along
and they went along
and they went along,
until they reached Foxy Loxy's cave.

In they all went
after Foxy Loxy.

From that day to this

Turkey Lurkey, Goosey Loosey,

Ducky Lucky, Cocky Locky,

and Henny Penny

have never been seen again.

And the King has never
been told the sky is falling.

But...

Foxy Loxy and Mrs. Foxy Loxy and their seven little foxes
still remember the fine feast they had that day.

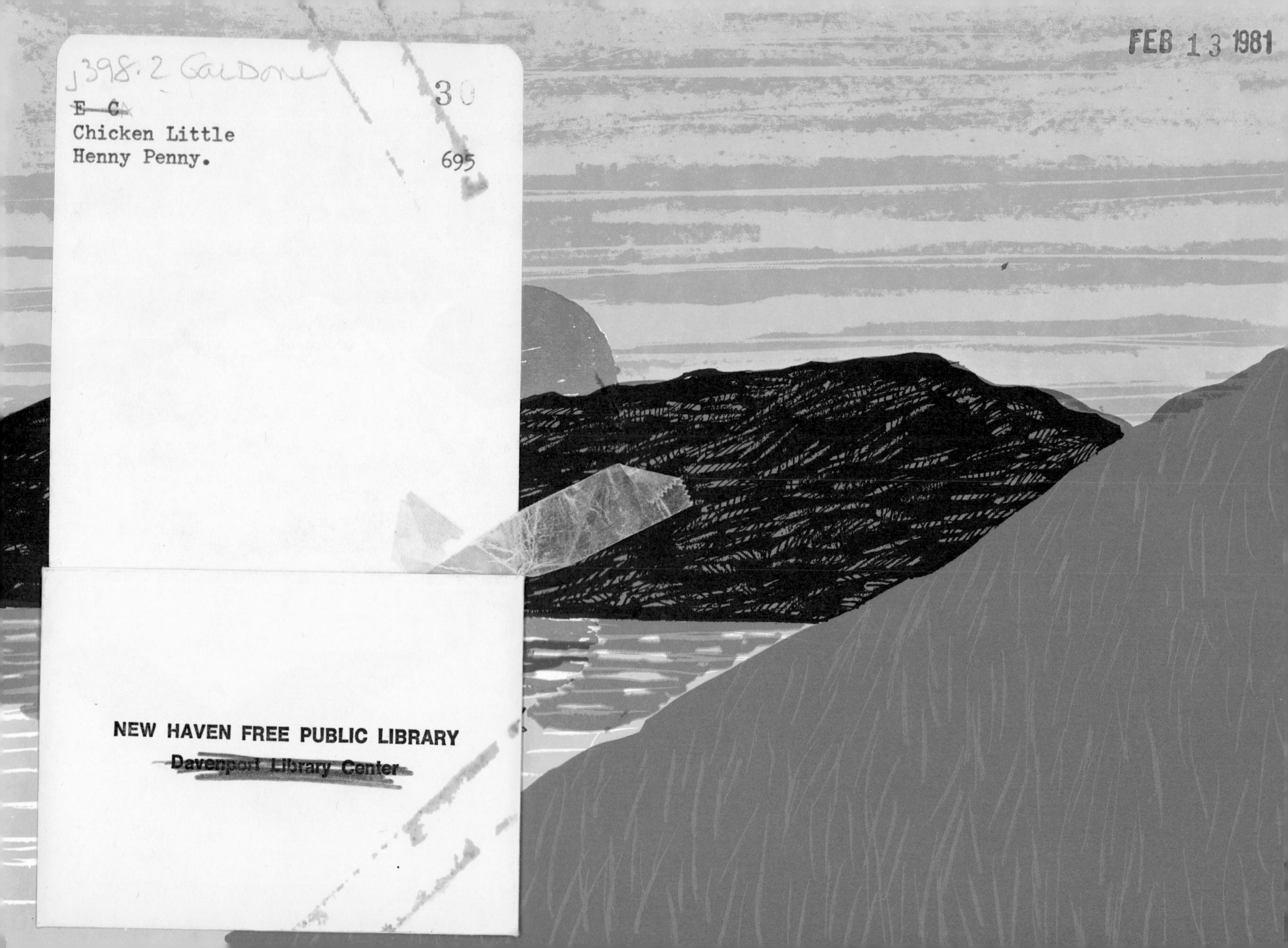